DREAMWORKS® **The PENGUINS** of **MADAGASCAR**™

nickelodeon™

WISHFUL THINKING

by Elizabeth Rudnick

Grosset & Dunlap
An Imprint of Penguin Group (USA) Inc.

GROSSET & DUNLAP
Published by the Penguin Group
Penguin Group (USA) Inc., 375 Hudson Street, New York, New York 10014, USA
Penguin Group (Canada), 90 Eglinton Avenue East, Suite
700, Toronto, Ontario M4P 2Y3, Canada
(a division of Pearson Penguin Canada Inc.)
Penguin Books Ltd., 80 Strand, London WC2R 0RL, England
Penguin Group Ireland, 25 St. Stephen's Green, Dublin 2, Ireland
(a division of Penguin Books Ltd.)
Penguin Group (Australia), 250 Camberwell Road, Camberwell, Victoria 3124, Australia
(a division of Pearson Australia Group Pty. Ltd.)
Penguin Books India Pvt. Ltd., 11 Community Centre,
Panchsheel Park, New Delhi—110 017, India
Penguin Group (NZ), 67 Apollo Drive, Rosedale, Auckland 0632, New Zealand
(a division of Pearson New Zealand Ltd.)
Penguin Books (South Africa) (Pty.) Ltd., 24 Sturdee Avenue,
Rosebank, Johannesburg 2196, South Africa

Penguin Books Ltd., Registered Offices: 80 Strand, London WC2R 0RL, England

ISBN 978-0-448-45867-0   10 9 8 7 6 5 4 3 2 1

WISHFUL THINKING

CHAPTER 1

It was a typical day at the New York Zoo. The elephant was washing off with his long trunk. The gorillas were eating bananas. The kangaroo was jumping around. And the Penguins were...listening to the radio!

To everyone who came to the zoo, Skipper, Kowalski, Private, and Rico looked like ordinary Penguins. But they weren't. They were an elite penguin force with one mission—keep the zoo safe! Skipper was the leader of the group while Kowalski thought of himself as the "mastermind." He was always making new inventions, but not all of them worked. The rest of the team was made up of Rico, who could cough up almost anything the team needed from his large stomach, and Private. Private loved to help but wasn't always the quickest penguin in the habitat.

At the moment, however, none of the members

of the elite penguin force were worried about the zoo's safety. They were trying to win a contest.

Inside the zookeeper's office, the four Penguins stood around a large radio on the desk. Kowalski tuned the dial with his flipper. There was a burst of static, and then music began playing.

"I've locked in on the frequency," Kowalski said proudly. The tall, thin penguin was always coming up with new inventions and ways to help the group.

Suddenly the music stopped and a long whistle sounded. Then a DJ's voice came over the air. "You know what that sound means: The lucky caller wins dinner at Senor Pete's Fish Hut!"

That was the announcement the Penguins had been waiting for. Skipper quickly karate chopped the phone he was standing next to. The receiver flew high into the air. In one swift move, Rico caught it while Private began dialing.

"Inputting code now!" Private said.

On the other end of the line, the phone began to ring. Then the DJ picked up.

No luck. They weren't the right caller. They dialed again.

"Sorry," the DJ said this time. "We already have a winner."

The Penguins were upset. It wasn't fair. They had done everything right! That meal was supposed to be theirs!

Letting out an angry growl, Rico threw the receiver down. But the penguin was stronger than he looked. The phone hit the table hard and then bounced back up—smacking Private right in the head!

"Oh!" Private cried. He stumbled backward and hit a jar of loose change. As the rest of his friends watched, he and the jar tumbled off the desk.

SMASH!

Quickly, the three Penguins jumped down off the desk. They had to make sure Private was all right. They found him buried under a pile of change. He pulled himself out and shook his head.

"Easy," Kowalski said. "You took a nasty knock to the cranium."

Skipper leaned closer. "What's your name, soldier?" he asked. He needed to make sure that Private wasn't badly hurt.

"Private," he answered.

"What's your rank?" Skipper asked.

"Private," he answered again.

Skipper asked one more thing. "What's your secret, hidden shame?"

"Private!" he said, a bit angrily. He was tired of all the questions.

Satisfied that his man was fine, Skipper turned back to the others. "We've got tracks to cover," he said, nodding at the coins and the jar. "Private, get rid of the evidence."

Private nodded. A penguin's job was never done.

A short time later, Private walked along one of the zoo's paths. In his arms, he carried a pile of coins. Private's load was so big, he didn't realize he was dropping a trail of pennies behind him.

"OW!"

Private stopped walking and cocked his head. *What was that?*

"OWWW!"

It sounded like someone was in pain.

"OWWWWWWWWW!"

The third cry brought Private to the zoo fountain. Mort the lemur was standing on the ledge surrounding it, biting into something shiny.

"OWWWWWWWWWW!" Mort screamed again. Then he pouted. "This gum ball is too ouchie!"

Private tried not to smile. "That isn't a gum ball," he said to the lemur. "It's a penny."

The lemur looked down at the shiny object in his hand. "Ohh," he said. Then he bit it again. "OWWWW!!! This penny is too ouchie!"

Private, being the kindhearted penguin that he was, didn't want Mort to keep hurting himself. Looking around, he tried to see if there was something to distract the small creature with. His eyes landed on the fountain. Aha! That was it!

"You know what you could do?" Private said, turning back to Mort. "You could toss the penny in the fountain and make a wish!"

Mort lowered the penny from his mouth. He looked thoughtful. "Could I wish for . . . gum balls?" he asked.

Private nodded. "Sure, Mort!" he said. His plan was working perfectly. It was harmless to make wishes in fountains, and it would keep Mort from hurting himself. "And then someday your wish will come true!" Private added for good measure.

"Okay!" Mort said excitedly. He walked closer to the fountain and pulled his arm back, ready to throw the penny. "I wish for"—he closed his eyes tight and tossed the penny toward the fountain—"gum balls!" The coin splashed into the water and sank to the bottom.

Opening his eyes, Mort looked around. "Where's my gum ball?" he asked, confused. "I want my gum ball!"

Once again, Private tried not to laugh. The silly lemur really believed that gum balls would just appear that second. "It doesn't happen right away," Private said. He was about to explain how a wish works when he suddenly stopped. Then his mouth fell open.

Mort was surrounded by gum balls!

Private closed his eyes and shook his head. Maybe he was just seeing things. But when he opened his eyes again, the gum balls were still there!

He had to tell the others about this—right away!

CHAPTER 2

Inside their secret lair, the other Penguins were relaxing when Private burst into the room.

"Skipper, Kowalski, Rico!" he cried breathlessly. "You won't believe this! The fountain is magic, and it's granting wishes!"

The three Penguins raised their eyebrows. Private was making no sense. Fountains didn't really grant wishes.

Did they?

It was time to find out the truth about fountains and wishes. Kowalski was ready to do the explaining.

As the others watched, he pulled down a large display chart. On the chart was a picture of a fountain, a birthday cake, and a falling star.

"Can wishes come true?" Kowalski asked as he pointed to the chart. He loved when he was in

charge and everyone had to listen. His voice grew more serious as he went on. "Do our hopes and dreams materialize if we just believe? Is there true magic in this mundane world of ours?"

Private jumped up. "Yes! Yes! Oh yes!" he cried.

"No!" Kowalski snapped. "Science does not allow for the existence of magic." He threw down the pointer stick and used his flipper to point at the chart. Then, as if to emphasize his point, he snapped the display chart, causing it to roll back up.

But Private shook his head. "Oh, Kowalski," he said. "If you'd just toss a penny in and make a wish, you'd see." He looked at his friend with big, innocent eyes.

Skipper looked back and forth between the two

Penguins. They clearly both believed they were right. There was only one way to put an end to this discussion.

They were going back to the fountain.

Moments later, the Penguins stood in front of the fountain. It looked like it always did. An ordinary fountain spurting ordinary water.

Muttering under his breath, Kowalski moved closer. He was holding a penny that Private had given him. "Utter frivolity," he said. But he made a wish. "I wish for a full-phase plasma blaster with repeating action and laser sights." Then he threw the penny into the fountain.

Nothing happened.

"There!" Kowalski cried. He began furiously stomping around. He had given up everything he believed in to make Private feel better about himself. And for what? Had he gotten a full-phase plasma blaster? No, he had ... suddenly, he tripped over something that looked an awful lot like a plasma blaster!

Wait a minute! His wish *had* come true! He had gotten a blaster! It was lying on the ground right in front of him! Before it could disappear, he snatched it up.

"Gah!" he shouted. "It's MAGIC!" He aimed at a lamppost and fired. The post dissolved in a blast of light, and Kowalski let out a crazy laugh.

"I told you! I told you!" Private cried, dancing over to him. "It's enchanted!" He, Rico, and Kowalski began doing a celebratory dance around the plasma blaster.

But their celebration was quickly stopped by Skipper.

"Yes, this is a wonderful, magical thing we've discovered," Skipper said. Then his tone grew darker. "But it could also be the worst thing that ever happened to us. One careless wish could lead to horrific disaster!"

"Like?" Kowalski asked, hugging his blaster close. He didn't see anything bad about the fountain.

"Like, I don't know . . . tidal waves! Or earthquakes! Or exposing our entire operation to the world,"

Skipper replied. "The risks are too great. So . . . I'm limiting you all to one small wish."

The others exchanged glances. That wasn't entirely fair. But Skipper had a point. If Kowalski could wish for—and get—a plasma blaster, there was no telling what could happen if the wishing got out of control.

With a nod from Skipper, Rico coughed up three coins. Skipper took one for himself and gave one to Private. The other one was Rico's.

Skipper held up his coin. He had only one wish. He had to think of something really good. "I'll wish for a, oh, I don't know," he said uncertainly. Finally he thought of something. "How about a fake mustache? Something for going incognito." Yes! That was it. The perfect wish! He threw his coin in the fountain.

Next up was Private. "Are day-boat scallops too much to ask for, Skipper?" Since they hadn't won the dinner contest, at least he could still get his favorite meal.

"Knock yourself out," Skipper said.

Private turned to say thank you, but Skipper wasn't there. In his place was a penguin with a mustache. "Ahh!" Private yelped. "Who are you?!"

"What have you done with Skipper?!" Kowalski shouted, while Rico let out a low *grrrr*.

The penguin held up his flipper. "Easy, boys, it's just me," he said as he took off the mustache to reveal that it was, in fact, Skipper. The fountain had worked again!

One by one, Private and Rico stepped up and made their wishes. Private asked for scallops while Rico thought long and hard before deciding on his wish—a Jet Ski.

And one by one, their wishes came true. Moments later Rico was Jet-Skiing around the habitat, while Private dined on delicious scallops. Kowalski experimented with the settings on his plasma blaster, and Skipper tried out different mustache styles. Everyone was content. And better yet, none of the wishes had been dangerous,

Now they just had to make sure that no one else found out about this fountain.

CHAPTER 3

In all his excitement to tell the others about the fountain, Private had forgotten one very important thing. Mort knew about the magic, too! And the little lemur wasn't very good at keeping secrets.

Inside the lemur habitat, King Julien sat on his throne. He was bored. And when he got bored, he liked to spy on the Penguins in the habitat next door. Tipping his crown back so the leaves didn't get in his eyes, he looked over. But what was this? Where had Rico gotten a Jet-Ski? He had always wanted a Jet-Ski, and he was king. He *should* have a Jet-Ski!

And when had the bossy one gotten a mustache? This was all entirely unfair! "I wonder where the penguin got such a wonderful disguise accessory," the king mused, turning to Maurice, his sergeant at arms.

Maurice shrugged. It wasn't his job to know where the Penguins shopped.

Nearby, Mort was chewing on a gum ball. He looked up. "Maybe the fountain," he suggested.

The king held back a laugh. Silly Mort. He was always saying the most ridiculous things. "How can a mustache come from a fountain?" the king asked, trying to be patient.

"It's a magic fountain," Mort replied, blowing a big bubble. "If you make a wish, it comes true."

King Julien's eyes grew wide, and he leaned forward on his throne. "Saywhatnow?" he asked breathlessly.

"Uh-huh," Mort said. "I wished for gum balls!" Smiling happily, he threw a handful of candy in the air.

King Julien smiled. This was interesting. Very, *very* interesting.

King Julien did not waste any time. With Maurice and Mort following close behind, Julien quickly made his way to the fountain. In his hand he held the necessary penny. But what could he wish for?

Wait a minute! He knew exactly what he could wish for!

"I wish for . . ." King Julien closed his eyes tight and raised his hands high in the air. Finally, he threw the penny. It flew up, up, up and then down, down, down. With a *plop*, it landed in the water. "In-line roller skates!" he finished.

The three lemurs leaned over and peered into the fountain. Nothing seemed to be happening.

"I am waiting, Mr. Fountain!" King Julien said loudly. "Where are my roller skates that are in a line?"

Still nothing.

With a sigh, King Julien turned to leave. "Eh, this is a bust. Let's go make fun of the chimpanzeezeezeezeees!"

He let out a loud screech as he took one step and lost his footing. Looking down, King Julien's eyes grew wide. He was wearing a pair of in-line roller skates! "Ah! Look! It is truthiness!" he shouted happily. "The fountain has granted my wish!"

As the king took a few skating steps forward, a grin spread across his face. This was the most exciting thing to happen in the zoo since his arrival. He had to share the news with everyone!

King Julien spread the news fast.

He rolled around the zoo and shouted, "The fountain! You throw in a penny, and it gives you things!"

Inside their habitat, the chimpanzees, Mason and Phil, looked at each other. A fountain that gave you things? They were going to have to see what this was all about.

King Julien kept on skating. "This is a magic-ness unlike any I have ever seen!" he said as he rolled by the gorillas, Bada and Bing.

"Magic?" Bada repeated, turning to Bing.

"This we gotta try!" Bing replied.

The lemur laughed. Yes! Everyone should try it. "And all you need is a penny!" he cried. "You can't say no to that price!"

Thanks to King Julien, in no time at all the animals in the zoo knew about the wishes.

A huge crowd had gathered around the fountain. Every animal there had coins that they began to toss into the water.

Plop!

"I wish for a new tire swing!" Bada said.

Not to be outdone by his fellow gorilla, Bing wished for five tons of bananas.

Plop!

Burt, the zoo's elephant, wished to go to Paris.

Plop!

Marlene the otter threw her coin in next. "A Spanish guitar that plays itself!" she wished.

Another *plop!* came as Roy the rhino threw his coin in. He wanted noise-canceling headphones.

As animal after animal made their wishes, King Julien skated around happily. Maurice followed behind carrying an armful of coins, and every few minutes Julien would throw one into the fountain and make a wish. *Plop.* "I want a new boomy box!" he shouted. *Plop, plop, plop, plop, plop.* "A secret admirer! Silky pajamas! A straw hat so I can play hilly-billy! A coffee mug that says 'World's Greatest King'! And . . . a new Maurice!"

Standing at a distance, Private watched as the lemur made wish after wish. He saw all the other animals throwing their coins into the fountain.

This was out of control! Skipper had been right. The fountain *was* dangerous.

He had to get back to Penguin Headquarters fast. It looked like the Penguins had a new mission!

CHAPTER 4

Inside Penguin Headquarters, the other Penguins were unaware of what was happening all around the zoo. In fact, they were still enjoying their own wishes from the fountain. Skipper in particular. Standing in front of a mirror, he took off the mustache. He looked at himself one way. Then another. "Yeah," he said, "that's pretty macho. But . . ." He slapped on the mustache again. "That's *muy, muy* macho!"

He was about to repeat the whole process when Private came rushing in.

"Skip—" he began and then stopped. Where was Skipper? And who was this strange penguin with a mustache?

Seeing the confused

look on Private's face, Skipper ripped off his disguise and asked what was wrong.

Ah! Now Private remembered! Skipper had wished for a mustache disguise. It really was a good wish. He would never get recognized if he went on a mission wearing the mustache. Maybe *he* should wish for a mustache . . . wait! No! Suddenly Private remembered why he had come rushing into the lair.

"*Everyone* knows about the fountain!" Private cried.

Skipper's eyes grew wide. This was bad. Very, *very* bad! They had to act fast. "Move out, men!" he ordered.

He turned, expecting to see the Penguins lining up. But they weren't there. Instead, Rico was standing in the middle of the room with an apple on his head. Kowalski was a few feet away, aiming his plasma blaster right at the apple.

"Aw, do we gotta?" Kowalski whined.

Skipper sighed. Sometimes being the leader of the group was exhausting. "Fine," he said. "Private and I will handle this."

Then, without another word, the two Penguins headed off. It was time to put an end to all this wishful thinking.

It didn't take too long for Skipper to see why Private had been worried. Aboveground, things were out of control. After finding a spot where they could observe unnoticed, the two Penguins scanned the zoo.

In the gorilla habitat, Bada was swinging wildly on his tire swing, while Bing stared at a large pile of bananas. There were so many, he didn't know where to begin eating. Meanwhile Marlene strolled along with a guitar that was playing itself. Passing by Roy, she didn't even seem to notice that the rhinoceros was wearing headphones.

"It's worse than I thought!" Skipper cried. "Who could have let our secret slip?"

Just then, King Julien skated up to them. He was wearing silk pajamas and a straw hat. In his hand

he held a mug that read #1 KING. "Checking it out, y'all," he said, giggling happily. "I am the world's greatest hilly-billy king in silky pajamas on skates!"

Aha! Skipper now knew *exactly* who had let the secret out. That pesky lemur! Letting out a big sigh, Skipper moved out of his spot. King Julien might have let the secret out, but it was going to be up to him to get that secret back in. And he was going to do it right now.

With Private's help, Skipper gathered all the zoo animals around the fountain.

"Now listen, folks," Skipper began. "I know everybody's jazzed to get their heart's desire. But we've got to talk about the elephant in the room."

At the word *elephant,* Private held up a postcard. There on the front was a picture of Burt. He was standing in the middle of a field in what looked like Paris, France. He was wearing a beret and carrying a bag full of baguettes. The front of the card read WISH YOU WERE HERE!

"Or," Skipper said, "should I say the elephant *not* in the room?! I'm telling you, keep wishing for all this stuff and, sooner or later, someone is going to notice."

As if on cue, Phil began signing frantically. He was seated on a lamppost and therefore had a better view than the others. Mason, noticing Phil's signing, jumped up. "Egad!" he cried. "Alice is coming!"

This was just what Skipper had been afraid of! If the zookeeper caught them or saw any of the animals with say, a pair of in-line skates, she would *definitely* know something was up. "Scatter!" he ordered. "Move!"

The animals quickly left the fountain. Some of them made it back to their homes, while others just went to find a place to hide. But there was one animal who was not moving quickly enough: Maurice.

Private was desperately trying to get the lemur away from the fountain. But the little, furry creature was weighed down by an armful of pennies. Private pushed Maurice, causing a few of the pennies to fall. But luckily, the push was enough to send the lemur behind a lamppost. The light hid the small creature.

Phew, Private thought. *That was—*

"What are you doing out of your habitat?" Alice asked.

Whoops!

Private had been so worried about making sure Maurice was hidden that he had left himself totally exposed. What was he going to do?

Suddenly he heard a hiss from under a bench nearby. It was Skipper!

"Serpentine slide!" he commanded.

Private didn't hesitate. He began moving like a snake, weaving first this way and then that. Alice gave chase.

"Come back here, you!" she shouted as Private slid along the ground. Then as Alice watched in awe, the penguin bounced onto a bench and over the brick wall in front of his habitat.

He had gotten away!

Under the bench, Skipper had watched the whole thing. "Aces, Private," he whispered. Then he focused back on the zookeeper. He didn't like her being so close to the fountain.

Alice shook her head. Those Penguins! They were constantly causing her trouble.

Turning to head back to her office, something shiny caught her eye. Bending down, she picked up a penny. As the light caught the coin, it shimmered, just like the water in the fountain.

Under the bench, Skipper gulped. She wouldn't. Would she? And then she did. Alice made a wish.

"Wish I knew what the story was with those Penguins," she said, throwing the penny into the water.

For a moment, nothing happened.

Then . . . *KA-BOOM!*

The zoo rocked with a loud explosion. When the ground stopped shaking, there was a huge hole—right in the middle of the penguin habitat.

Penguin Headquarters had been revealed!

Kowalski and Rico looked stunned. "Wow!" Kowalski said. "That turbo setting packs a punch!"

Rico coughed up dust and shrugged.

Then, through the silence after the explosion,

they heard a noise. It sounded a lot like a human gasping.

Slowly, the two Penguins looked up. Then they gulped. Standing there, staring straight at them, was Alice.

"Th-th-the Penguins!" she stammered. "They've got a whole secret lair down there! With weapons! I KNEW THOSE PENGUINS WERE UP TO SOMETHING!"

Kowalski and Rico exchanged glances. Skipper had been right all along. And now, it looked like it was the Penguins who were in real danger!

CHAPTER 5

Night had fallen over the zoo. But it was far from quiet. As soon as Alice had discovered the Penguin's headquarters, she had alerted the zoo authorities.

Soon a fleet of helicopters swept down and began circling above while spotlights swung back and forth scanning the grounds. Outside the gates, a crowd had gathered, eager to find out what was going on.

Suddenly several long ropes dropped out of the helicopters. Then animal control officers climbed down. As soon as their boots hit the ground, they raced off. They needed to find those Penguins!

Hiding under one of the zoo's benches, the Penguins watched all the action. Luckily, and using some clever maneuvers, they had managed to escape while Alice was calling in help. But the situation wasn't good.

"We've been compromised, men!" Skipper

whispered. It was time to take action. This is what they had been trained for. "Maneuver Delta Tango Victor!"

Each Penguin took a deep breath.

They narrowed their eyes.

Then in one smooth motion, all four Penguins slid out from under the bench.

CLANG! CLANG! CLANG! CLANG!

Before they knew what was happening, four cages had been slammed down on top of them.

"Dang!" Skipper cried as he felt his cage lifted up. "Should have gone with Delta Tango Foxtrot."

The Penguins had been captured. And it was big news! Everyone in the city wanted to hear the story, and Chuck Charles, the local news anchor, was ready to tell them.

"A startling discovery that rocks the very understanding of human/animal relations," he said, standing in front of the destroyed penguin habitat.

Behind him, Alice leaned close to another news anchor as she told her side of the story. "I always knew something was off about those Penguins," she said.

Turning back to the main camera, Chuck Charles finished his report. "The Penguins will be taken to a government lab where they will be studied and painfully dissected."

Meanwhile, the Penguins were still on the zoo grounds. An animal control officer was pushing the caged animals away on a cart. He had been ordered to get them to the lab as soon as possible.

Sitting inside their cages, the Penguins were silent. They were each lost in their own thoughts.

Skipper was thinking that this was one big mess. And he had tried to warn everyone. But as usual, no one had listened. If they ever got out of these cages and back to the zoo, he was going to have a serious talk with the other animals. Next time, they would know better.

Private was worried. He had heard that news anchor. He didn't know exactly what dissecting was, but he knew it didn't sound good. He started to wish that he had eaten more scallops while he could, but then he stopped himself. Wishing was what got them in trouble in the first place. Sighing, he hung his head.

Kowalski on the other hand was more worried about the plasma blaster that had been so rudely taken from him.

And Rico? Well, Rico wasn't thinking about much.

Suddenly the cart hit a bump, jarring the Penguins. Snapping out of his silence, Skipper glanced around at the others. Then he narrowed his eyes and glared at Kowalski. "You *had* to try the turbo setting?!?"

Kowalski shrugged. "Sorry, sorry," he said. "You know I can't resist overkill!"

Before Skipper could respond, Private spoke up. "Don't blame Kowalski," the penguin said softly. "This is all my fault! What with all this wishing business."

It was true. Or at least, Private *thought* it was all his fault. After all, he had been the one to tell Mort to make a wish in the first place. If he hadn't done that, the fountain's powers would never have been known. Private wouldn't have told the others, so Kowalski wouldn't have wished for a plasma blaster. King Julien would never have seen Mort with all his gum balls and wondered where he had gotten them. Mort never would have told him, so

Julien never would have made all his wishes. In turn, the king wouldn't have told *everyone* in the zoo, and they wouldn't have *all* made their own silly wishes.

Private let out another sigh. There was no way around it. This *was* his fault, and he didn't know how to fix it.

Or did he?

At that very moment, the four caged Penguins were being carried past the fountain. Private had an idea! He was going to save the day! If all this trouble had started because of wishes, why couldn't it *stop* because of wishes?

"Quickly, Rico!" Private shouted. "Give me a penny!"

The other Penguin nodded and immediately coughed up one shiny penny. Private reached over and grabbed it. They were passing the fountain. Time was running out. He had to act fast.

The others, who quickly realized what Private was doing, grabbed hold of their cage bars. "Only one shot, Private," Skipper said. "Make it count!"

Private nodded. He took a deep breath. "I wish none of this had ever happened!" he cried. Then, closing his eyes, he threw the penny.

It tumbled through the air, head over tails,

over and over again. As the Penguins watched in horror, the penny came down and hit the edge of the fountain. Then with a *ping* it flipped up, up, up. Just when it looked like the penny was going to land on the ledge of the fountain and stop . . .

the Penguins held their breaths.

The penny began to wobble and teeter. It spun a bit closer to the edge. Then a bit closer, until finally, *PLOP!* The penny fell into the water.

"YES!" Private shouted just as there was a bright burst of light and then everything went a little bit . . . crazy.

CHAPTER 6

Private stuck his head out from under a pile of coins. He looked around. He was in Alice's office. The sun was shining, and his friends were all standing around him with worried looks on their faces.

"Easy," Kowalski said. "You took a nasty knock to the cranium."

Wait a second—that sounded very familiar.

"What's your name, soldier?" Skipper asked.

That sounded familiar, too! "Pri—" he began to answer and then stopped. "Wait, what? I . . . I'm back!"

He leaped up, scattering coins everywhere. His

plan had worked! When he had tossed the penny in the fountain and made his wish, it had come true. No one had ever discovered the magic of the fountain, which meant no one made silly wishes, and no one had managed to uncover the Penguins' secret lair! Everything was back to normal!

Private danced around happily. "My wish came true!" he giggled. "None of it ever happened!"

As Private continued to dance around, the other three Penguins exchanged looks. That knock to the head must have been harder than they thought. Private was making even less sense than usual!

A short while later, the Penguins made their way home. Private had tried to explain everything that happened, but Skipper, Kowalski, and Rico had no memory of the fountain. In fact, Kowalski had a different explanation for what Private had experienced.

"What really happened," Kowalski said as they walked past the elephant enclosure, "was the concussive force to your brain triggered an elaborate, deluded fantasy."

"So it was all a dream?" Private asked.

The other penguin nodded. "Absolutely. As I said, wishes aren't real."

Private let out a sigh. If Kowalski said they weren't true, they probably weren't. After all, he was the smart one. Still, it would have been pretty amazing to have a wishing fountain ...

Suddenly Private stopped. He had just passed Burt. And he could have sworn the elephant was holding a baguette in his trunk. As the others continued to walk, Private turned and made his way back. His eyes grew wide. Sure enough, Burt was standing there wearing a beret and holding a baguette.

The elephant shrugged. "What?" he asked.

It looked like Kowalski might have a bit more explaining to do about wishes and magic fountains.

DREAMWORKS The PENGUINS of MADAGASCAR
nickelodeon

BRUSH WITH DANGER

The New York Zoo was a busy place. Parents and children wandered the paths between animal habitats, looking at the elephant and the gorillas, the lemurs and the kangaroos. Vendors selling hot dogs and ice cream were busy putting on ketchup and mustard or scooping out vanilla and chocolate. And all along the paths there were benches so people could sit down and enjoy the day.

On this particular day, though, one of the benches was out of service. Alice, the zookeeper, was busy painting a bench right outside one of the habitats. She had her headphones on and was singing quite loudly—and off-key. People walking by winced but kept going. There were animals to see.

A man and woman stopped in front of the bench. They were staring at the zoo map trying to figure out where to go next.

"Okay," the woman said, "we've seen the rhino, the otter, and the Penguins . . ."

The man cut her off. "Hey, wasn't there something weird about those Penguins?" he said.

"What do you mean?" the woman asked, tilting her head. The Penguins hadn't seemed weird to her. They just seemed like ordinary, black-and-white creatures playing in their zoo home.

The man didn't seem convinced. "Were they doing . . . tae kwon do?" he asked.

Nearby, two of the very Penguins the man was talking about were hiding behind the trunk of a tree. Skipper and Rico had been following the couple ever since they had stopped in front of their habitat.

Because the man was right. They *had* been doing tae kwon do. And the woman was wrong.

They were *not* ordinary Penguins. They were an elite penguin force based in the zoo with one mission—keep the zoo safe. The team was made up of four Penguins. Skipper was the leader, while Kowalski was the self-proclaimed "mastermind" of the group. Private was, well, Private. He helped when he could but often got the group into trouble . . . accidentally. And then there was Rico. The fourth Penguin didn't say much, but he had a unique gift: He could cough up anything they needed from his very large and apparently bottomless gut. That little trick had come in handy on more than one occasion.

Together, the four Penguins had prevented disaster time and time again. But it was very important that their identities were not revealed. People—especially Alice the zookeeper—had to believe that they were just like every animal in the zoo. Ordinary.

Which was why they'd followed the couple who had spotted their somewhat suspicious behavior back at the habitat. Skipper felt responsible. He had given the order to do a few minutes of tae kwon do training. He hadn't realized that they were being watched. Now he needed to fix it.

"He knows too much," Skipper said to Rico. The other Penguin was holding a blow-dart stick in his flipper. "Take your shot."

Rico took a deep breath and raised the blow dart.

Then, just as he was about to exhale, the woman playfully waved off the man's concerns.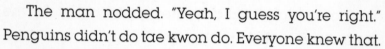

"That's crazy talk," she said, smiling.

The man nodded. "Yeah, I guess you're right." Penguins didn't do tae kwon do. Everyone knew that.

Skipper heard the man and let out a sigh of relief. *Phew!* Crisis averted. The Penguins' secret was safe. But wait! Rico was still about to fire. Reaching over, Skipper knocked down the dart gun just as Rico let out one mighty breath.

The dart flew out of the stick and through the air. As Skipper and Rico watched, it bounced off one of the habitat walls and changed direction. Then before the Penguins could do anything to stop it, the dart hit Alice . . . right in the behind! Jumping up, she let out a squeak. Her eyes widened. And then, with her paintbrush still in hand, she sank to the ground, unconscious.

Burt, the zoo's elephant, had witnessed the entire thing from his nearby habitat. Reaching his long trunk over the wall, he grabbed Alice's paintbrush. He lifted it in front of his eyes and took a good, long look. Then he smiled. "Ahh," he said, "I've always wanted to dabble in the visual arts." After turning around, he went to the far wall of his habitat and began to paint.

From their spot by the tree, Skipper and Rico exchanged a glance. This wasn't good.

"Bug out!" Skipper ordered.

Rico nodded. Quickly, they raced away. By the time Alice woke up, the two Penguins would be safely back in their habitat. She would never know what had happened. They hoped.

A little while later, Alice woke up. She shook her head. Why did she feel so sleepy? And why was she on the ground in front of the elephant habitat? Last thing she remembered, she had been painting. Then something had stung her, and it all went blank.

As she started to push herself to her feet, her eyes grew wide. A large crowd had gathered in front of her. *That's nice of them*, she thought. *I didn't know so many people care.*

"I'm okay," she told the crowd. "I'm okay."

But the crowd didn't actually seem concerned. In fact, they were staring at something behind her. Slowly, she turned around. Alice's eyes grew wide again.

True, a huge crowd had gathered. But they were not worried about Alice. They were intrigued by what was going on inside Burt's habitat. As Alice stood rooted to her spot, there were *ooh*s and *aah*s and an occasional clap. A few people were pointing, and everyone looked amazed.

And they had every reason to be.

Along one of the habitat's walls, Burt had created a painting of an elephant. The bright-yellow color was almost comical, and it was a bit childish in design, but the crowd loved it.

"Have you ever seen such talent?" one woman said.

"That is art!" another man cried. "I would pay top dollar to have one of those hanging in my loft."

As the people continued to compliment his work, Burt blissfully swiped his brush along the wall. He liked all the attention. But he liked painting even more!

CHAPTER 2

Inside their secret lair beneath the habitat, the Penguins were very busy—playing a game of cards. After all, as Skipper often said, even elite penguin forces needed time to relax every once in a while.

Skipper, Private, and Rico were sitting at a round table with cards in their flippers. In front of them was a pile of fish they had been using to bet along with Private's prized Lunacorn. Kowalski was the only penguin not partaking in the game. He was too busy working on one of his many plans—or so he had told Skipper when Skipper had asked him to play.

At the moment, the tall, skinny penguin was hunched over his workstation on the opposite side of the lair from where the others were playing cards. The lair was full of sophisticated equipment and training devices to keep the force on top of its game. If any of the humans walking through the zoo ever found out about the lair, it would be disastrous. Luckily, that hadn't happened. Well, it *almost* had once, but that was a whole different story. For the time being, the Penguins were safe in their underground hideout.

Suddenly Kowalski stood up straight. Then he threw his flippers in the air and spun around to face the others. "I've done it!" he shouted triumphantly.

Skipper, Private, and Rico looked up from their cards. What was Kowalski talking about this time? The tall penguin was always coming up with new plans or creating devices. It wasn't unusual for him to cry out things like "I've done it!" or "This is the one!" But more often than not, the inventions didn't work—or at least not the way they were supposed to.

Kowalski went on. "I've just designed a pocket hyperbolic quantum accelerator that will save civilization!" He gave the others a huge grin and puffed out his chest proudly.

"Well," Skipper said after a moment, "that earns a big 'attaboy.'" He figured it was good to support his number one scientific team member—even if things didn't always work out. Just as Skipper was going to add another line of praise, Kowalski put his flippers on his hips. Uh-oh. This wasn't good. Neither was the serious look he gave them. "There is, however," he went on grimly, "a fifty percent chance the pocket hyperbolic quantum accelerator could actually *destroy* civilization."

"I see one major problem with your invention," Skipper said to Kowalski. "We don't have pockets." To prove Skipper's point, Rico attempted to put his flippers in his pockets. But as he had said, there was nowhere to put them.

Next to him, Private was thinking there was a problem with the invention, too. But it had nothing to do with the fact that he couldn't stuff his flippers into any pockets. Even though beside him, Rico was still trying awfully hard to find a way. No, Private saw a slightly different issue.

"Couldn't the fifty percent chance of worldwide destruction be a problem, too?" he said.

Skipper raised an eyebrow. Private had a point. Maybe it would be better if the device was destroyed. "Rico," he said, turning to the demolitions expert of the group, "what do you think?"

The penguin nodded. He agreed. The device should be destroyed. Quickly he made his way over to Kowalski's worktable, and letting out a loud *hork,*

he coughed up a hammer. Then he lifted it up. *Slam!* He smashed the device flat.

When he was done doing that, he picked up the flattened object and raced over to the lair's boiler. Before Kowalski could utter a squeak of protest, Rico opened the boiler doors and threw the broken device into the flames. He slammed the door shut and waited. When he thought it was ready, he opened the doors back up. The device was now nothing more than a pile of ashes. Coughing up a cup, he poured the ashes into it. Then, as the other Penguins watched, he rushed over to Kowalski. Stopping in front of the tall penguin, Rico tilted the cup and poured the ashes out.

There was a moment of silence. Finally, Kowalski spoke. "Yeah," he said dryly. "That was my new calculator."

Oops!

"Rico," Skipper said, looking at his demolitions expert. "Destroy the right device this time. Maybe destroy them all, just to be sure."

The penguin nodded and saluted his leader. Turning, he started to make his way back to Kowalski's workstation.

"Wait!" Kowalski said, stopping Rico. "There is no device to destroy. I haven't built it yet."

The others looked confused. Then what had he just been talking about?

Kowalski went on. "It's just a plan," he explained. "A very *big* plan."

From behind his back, Kowalski pulled down a screen and revealed a large and intricate drawing. There were lines and random letters and shapes all over it.

Skipper and Private tilted their heads. They

squinted their eyes. Nothing. They couldn't make out anything in front of them.

"Oh! That's different," Skipper finally said. "Plans aren't dangerous."

Standing next to him, Rico slumped down. He was disappointed. He'd been looking forward to destroying some more things.

"Unless . . . ," Skipper said, causing Rico to perk up. "They fall into the wrong hands!"

That was just what Rico had hoped to hear! He began moving closer to Kowalski, ready to take the plans and dispose of them.

Kowalski jerked back. "No!" he shouted. "I've wasted the best years of my lonely, lonely life on these plans. I won't let you destroy them!" Then, to prove just how much the plans meant to him, Kowalski leaned over and gave them a big, fat kiss.

If Rico was going to destroy those plans, it looked like he'd have to get by Kowalski first. And that wasn't going to be easy.

CHAPTER
3

Meanwhile, outside Burt the elephant's habitat, a large crowd had gathered. Men, women, and children *ooh*ed and *aah*ed as they looked at several easels displaying the elephant's abstract paintings.

Looking at the crowd, Alice smiled. This was exactly what she had wanted to happen. As soon as word had gotten out that there was an elephant who could paint, the crowds had started flocking. Everyone wanted their chance to see this rare event.

"Postcard reproductions are for sale in the Zoovenir Shop," Alice said, walking back and forth in front of the habitat. Then she paused dramatically before adding, "*Shhh* . . . the *artiste* approaches."

Turning, she watched with the crowd as Burt walked over to a blank canvas set up inside his habitat. The elephant was wearing a beret—in an elephant size. As the crowd watched in awe, Burt picked up a brush with his trunk. Then he dipped it in some paint.

"Hmmm," he murmured as he looked at the canvas. He needed to put this first brush in exactly the right spot. Then he saw it. The spot where he would start his next masterpiece. With great care, he drew the brush across the canvas—and created a plain, black line.

The crowd let out a collective, "Ooooooooo . . ."

Burt drew another black line. "Ahhhhhh . . . ," the crowd gasped.

Then he added a red squiggle in the middle. The crowd went wild. As he continued to paint, Burt paid no attention to the crowd. But they were watching him closely. They followed every swish he made, so it looked as though the whole crowd was swaying back and forth.

Observing the people's reactions, Alice's smile grew wider. She couldn't help it—she was in awe of the painting elephant, too. Who knew an animal at her zoo could have such a hidden talent!

///// ///// /////

Back in Penguin Headquarters, Kowalski was still trying to keep his plans safe. Skipper and Rico were eager to get rid of the drawing that could potentially save the world—or destroy it. But Kowalski would not step away from the plans. He used his black-and-white body to block them as Rico moved closer.

Skipper gave him a stern look. "Kowalski," he began, "I don't relish global Armageddon . . ." As leader of an elite penguin force he didn't *want* war of any kind, but if it *were* to happen, there was one aspect of Armageddon that he wouldn't mind: "The part with the mutant vampire motorcycle gangs that rule the vast wastelands. Looking forward to throwing down with those boys . . ." Skipper drifted off as he pictured himself racing neck and neck with a vampire on a motorcycle.

"Skipper?" Private's voice broke into the daydream.

Snapping back to reality, Skipper got back to the point. Kowalski's plans. "But on the other hand, I look at that scribble, and it's just so much . . . gobbledygook."

Kowalski crossed his flippers and looked hurt. "Life's work, Skipper," he pointed out—again.

"Anyway," Skipper went on, ignoring Kowalski, "save it or shred it. You make the call."

This was a turn of events. Kowalski had been sure Skipper would just destroy it. No questions asked. But now it was up to *him* to decide.

He began to pace back and forth in front of the plans, a grim look on his face. "Should I destroy my greatest creation and deprive civilization of something wonderful?" He was talking more to himself than to the other Penguins. "Or keep it and risk total global annihilation?"

Watching their friend pace, Private leaned over to Skipper. "I have never seen him so conflicted," he said softly.

Skipper shook his head. Unfortunately,

he had. Just yesterday in fact. At the snow cone booth. Kowalski had paced back and forth in front of the booth just like he was doing now. And he had had the same grim look on his face.

"Should I indulge myself with the luscious but familiar flavors of a blueberry bubblegum?" he had asked himself. "Or do I venture into the high risk/high reward of honeydew lemon?"

Yesterday's dilemma had been small in comparison to today's. Yet Kowalski was just as stressed then as he was now.

Skipper and Private turned their attention back to the other Penguin. They were about to put an end to the pacing when there was a loud noise from above them.

"What's the ruckus?" Skipper asked.

Private shrugged. He didn't know. But he wanted to find out. Leaving Kowalski with his plans, Skipper, Private, and Rico raced out of the lair.

In moments, the three Penguins arrived topside. What they saw made their jaws drop. Crowds of people were crammed into the zoo! More were at the entrance waiting to get in, and a news crew had set up its cameras to get all the action. Overhead, a helicopter approached, its propellers whirring. And

there, in the center of the ruckus, was Burt and his paintings.

Stepping directly in front of the elephant's pen, local news anchor Chuck Charles raised his microphone. He began his report.

"Chuck Charles here," he said, smiling brightly. "Live at the zoo with the art world's latest sensation: a pachyderm with a penchant for painting."

Suddenly, the helicopter swooped lower, its propellers kicking up dirt and blowing people's hair around.

"Arriving on the scene now is famed art critic Bella Bon Bueno," Chuck Charles explained as the helicopter landed. A woman stepped out and looked around. She had her nose in the air and looked every inch the snooty art critic.

Chuck Charles made his way to her side and once again held up his microphone. "Tell us, Bella," he said, "is Burt the elephant the next Pandy Warhol?" Pandy Warhol had been the last big name in animal painters.

Bella lifted her sunglasses. She narrowed her eyes at Chuck. Then she replied, "The panda was a hack."

Watching from the island in the middle of their habitat, Skipper, Private, and Rico took in Bella's arrival and the growing crowd. Right now the situation seemed in control, and there was no pressing danger. But Skipper wanted to wait it out to be sure. You never knew when a crowd could turn ugly.

Just as Skipper was in the middle of creating an elaborate plan for *if* things went wrong, Kowalski emerged from the lair. He was still holding the plans in his flipper.

"Gentlemen," he began dramatically, "you are right." He drew the diagram close to his chest. "If these plans were to fall into the wrong hands, civilization itself would come to an end. Therefore, they must be destroyed."

As Kowalski spoke, the helicopter slowly began to lift off the ground.

Skipper nodded. "Good move, Kowalski," he said. "Nice to see you siding with civilization."

And then something terrible happened. As the helicopter rose higher above the zoo, the wind from its propellers began whipping faster and faster. Suddenly, a big gust blew over the Penguins' habitat, and before Kowalski could do anything, the plans were ripped out of his flippers!

The Penguins watched helplessly as the plans flew up, up, up. In moments, they were completely out of their reach.

This couldn't happen! They had to get them back—or else civilization was in grave danger!

"Pursue those plans!" Skipper ordered.

Together, the four Penguins flipped off the island and out of their habitat. It was time to save the world—again.

CHAPTER 4

Unaware of the danger her helicopter had caused, Bella Bon Bueno was busy inspecting Burt's paintings. Alice had placed them on easels and then lined them up to make it easier to view them. Bella approached the first one.

She leaned in close. Then she stepped away. Then she leaned in close again. As they watched her review the elephant's work, Burt held his breath and Alice stood with her hands on her hips.

For a moment, it seemed as though Bella liked the first one ... until she wrinkled her nose in disgust. Then she let out a dismissive *sniff.*

She did *not* like the first painting.

Burt and Alice let out disappointed sighs. This was not the reaction they had been looking for. Maybe she would feel differently about the next painting.

But she didn't.

And she didn't like the next one, either.

It was beginning to look like Burt's fifteen minutes of fame were up. There was only one more painting to review. If she sniffed at that one, Burt would have to put down his paintbrush forever.

While Bella had been busy turning up her nose at Burt's paintings, the Penguins had been busy trying to track the runaway plan. They had followed it out of the habitat, over the crowds, and then watched helplessly as it began to drift down ever so slowly—landing on top of the last of Burt's displayed paintings and covering it completely.

Sneaking behind a tree, the Penguins hunched low and waited to see what would happen. There was a lot at stake. If that plan somehow got out of the pen before the Penguins could retrieve it, who knew who might see it. An evil mastermind could figure out its true meaning—and destroy the world!

Turning to review the last painting, Bella wore the same bored expression on her face that she had for all the other paintings. But as soon as she saw the painting—or rather, Kowalski's plans—her eyes grew wide. Then she clasped her hands together in glee and gasped with joy. Holding one hand near her heart, she reached out as if to touch the painting, an excited smile on her face.

"What's this one?!" she finally exclaimed. "The elephant is going in a bold, new direction here . . . geee-nius!"

Inside the pen, Burt looked confused. But that wasn't even his painting!

Then Bella Bon Bueno made her final critique. "This *must* go straight to the museum for all the world to savor."

Watching from their spot behind the tree, the four Penguins gulped. Their worst fear was about to come true. The plan was going to leave the zoo!

A short while later, the Penguins had gathered back at the lair. Kowalski was miserable. His big plan, his life work, was gone. Taken away from him by a horrible twist of fate.

Private didn't like seeing his friend so sad. He tried to think of something he could say to make him feel better. "On the bright side, Kowalski," he finally said, "your work is the buzz of the art scene."

Kowalski shook his head. "Sure, the perfect symmetry of my equation may look like a harmless abstract," he said. "But any evil genius with a Vandyke will see the truth."

To prove his point, he whipped out a bowling

pin. He had drawn an evil genius face on the pin, complete with a mustache and small patch of hair on the chin. Then, as the others watched, he waddled over to his chalkboard. Kowalski had drawn a small-scale version of his plan.

"Let me illustrate," Kowalski continued. He scrunched his face and made his voice sound evil. "I am an evil genius visiting the museum."

Private grinned. He liked playing make-believe! Grabbing his stuffed Lunacorn, he made the horned animal walk into the museum as well. "Hello there," Private said in a high-pitched "Lunacorn" voice. "I'm visiting the museum, too. Can you help me find a rainbow painting?"

Skipper gave Private a stern look.

"Private," Skipper ordered. "Stay on message."

With a sigh, Private put down his Lunacorn. When he was once again focused, Kowalski continued. "As I was saying . . ." The penguin's voice once again became deeper. "I'm an evil genius visiting the museum. I wish I had a pocket hyperbolic quantum accelerator that I could use to destroy the world."

Kowalski walked the bowling pin past the "painting." Then he had the bowling pin stop and turn. Aha! The bowling pin/evil genius had just spotted something! A plan to destroy the world—right there in the museum. Kowalski threw his head back and let out an evil laugh, just like an evil genius would do.

Skipper shuddered. Kowalski was right. If the plan did make it to the museum it would only be a matter of time before something like this happened. "That diagram must never see the light of track lighting," he finally said.

They had to get that plan back—and fast!

CHAPTER 5

It didn't take long for the Penguins to put together a plan. Grabbing what they needed, they snuck out of the zoo and made their way to the museum. Then they jumped up on one another's shoulders until they looked like a penguin totem poll. For the final touch, they put on a long, gray trench coat and a hat. Then they made their way up to the admissions booth.

But their disguise didn't work. They asked for a child's ticket, but the ticket vendor took one look and knew there was no child anywhere. Then they asked for a senior ticket. That didn't work, either. Finally, the vendor had a security guard come and escort the "man" out of the museum. Unfortunately, as they were led out, the guard accidently pulled their coat

off. The Penguins quickly left the admissions office, leaving a confused security guard behind.

Since going in the front door was out of the question, the Penguins needed a Plan B. Luckily, Kowalski loved to come up with plans. Quickly, he formulated a new mission. The museum had air-conditioning. Air-conditioning meant air ducts. They could crawl into the museum through one of them and never be spotted! As soon as Kowalski filled the others in on their next move, they made their way back to the museum and into one of the main air ducts. "Ventilation shaft," Skipper observed as the four Penguins walked single file through the narrow, metal tubing. "Seems a tad cliché."

Behind him, Kowalski rolled his eyes. "Ahh, cliché," he said. "French for *I don't hear anyone else coming up with anything.*"

In the museum gallery below, a security guard stood next to the air-conditioning panel. He was getting hot. And unaware that an elite penguin force had infiltrated the air ducts, he turned the AC down. In the vent above, wind suddenly began to blow— hard. Before they could do anything, the four Penguins were pushed back, back, back. *Clank!* They hit the end of the vent. Then *bang!* They blew through the outside duct. And finally, *splat!* They landed in a heap on the ground outside the museum.

"What's French for *This ain't happenin?*" Skipper said as the others groaned.

Kowalski shrugged sheepishly. "Touché," he replied.

It was time to come up with Plan C.

By the time the Penguins came up with a third— and hopefully final—plan, night had almost fallen. This time, the Penguins weren't taking any chances. They couldn't go in the front and they couldn't make it through the air ducts, but maybe, just maybe, they could go in through the back.

The plan was simple—a classic really. The Penguins were going to sneak into the museum inside the hollow belly of a horse statue. It was called a Trojan horse because a long, long time ago, soldiers from one army had snuck into the other army's territory by hiding in a huge horse statue. Skipper figured if it had worked for those guys, it should work for them.

So they found a wooden Trojan horse, pushed it right up to the loading entrance of the museum, knocked on the door, and then jumped inside to wait. A moment later a security guard opened the door. Seeing the horse, he shrugged and pulled it inside.

When the horse had come to a stop and the security guard had left, the Penguins flipped on their flashlight. They were crammed together in the small space.

"It worked?" Kowalski said in disbelief.

"But isn't this a cliché, too?" Private asked.

Skipper raised his head. Or at least he tried to. It was pretty tight inside the horse. "Nah," he answered. "It's a classic."

"Why is that?" Kowalski asked.

"Because it was *my* idea," Skipper replied matter-of-factly.

Now they just had to wait until the museum closed. Then they could sneak out, grab the plan, and get back to the lair.

Finally it was time. They tumbled out of the horse and made their way to the gallery where the plan was supposed to be displayed. Sure enough, it was right where it was supposed to be. It had been framed and hung on a wall. For a moment, Kowalski just stared at it proudly.

Then Private moved in to grab the plan. He was just about to touch it when Skipper stopped him. "Not so fast," the leader said. He signaled to Rico, who coughed up a smoke bomb. Then as the others watched in horror, Skipper threw the bomb into the air where it exploded.

But Skipper wasn't crazy. He was proving a point. As the smoke trickled down, it revealed a complex web of red laser beams. It was an invisible alarm system! He nodded. "Just as I suspected. Kowalski, options?"

The tall Penguin thought for a moment. "How do you feel about disco?" he finally said.

Skipper shrugged. "Ambivalent. Why?"

He got his answer when Rico coughed up a tape player and sparkly disco ball. He pressed Play, and loud disco music began echoing through the room. Then Private jumped onto the sparkly ball, followed by Rico, Kowalski, and finally Skipper. When everyone was on the ball, it looked like an odd penguin-shaped totem pole. As the music played, Skipper's head moved to the beat, Kowalski grooved, Rico nodded, and Private's flippers flapped while his feet moved the ball forward—right into the path of the red beams. But that was the plan! As soon as the ball got within the laser field, red beams hit it and began shooting off in every direction. It was a diversion! If they could keep the ball moving forward, they would be safe.

As the music continued to play, the four Penguins rolled their way closer and closer to the wall and Kowalski's plan.

Unfortunately, Rico was having a bit of trouble. He missed a beat and accidently got a burn on his backside. But with a warning from Skipper, he quickly found the rhythm again and continued on. Rico wouldn't let his team down because of a teeny, tiny injury.

Finally, just as the song came to an end, they reached the plan. Jumping off the ball, they all stopped and stared at the drawing framed on the wall. Finally, Skipper reached up, eager to take the

plan down and get out of there. "Okay," he said, "time to shred this puppy."

Suddenly, Kowalski stepped in front of Skipper. "I can't let you do that," he said.

Skipper didn't understand. What was going on? Just moments ago, Kowalski had been with them. He had admitted it wasn't safe to have the plan out there. Now he was changing his mind? Why?

"Look," Kowalski went on. "Its subtle symmetry of form makes it a truly unique piece of art. It would be a crime to destroy it." His voice had grown serious.

The other Penguins looked at Kowalski. Then they looked at the diagram. He had a point. They began to nod their heads in agreement.

"It is rather . . . subtle," Private said, "in, you know, a unique, symmetryish way."

Rico agreed.

Finally, Skipper spoke. "Maybe," he said slowly. "*But* we just can't leave it here where any odd wondering mad scientist with a Vandyke could discover it."

The others were silent as they contemplated Skipper's words. He, too, had a point. But what could they do?

Suddenly, Rico coughed up a pencil. Then, walking over to the plan, he erased one tiny plus sign from it. As the others watched, he filled in the empty space with a drawing of the Lunacorn.

"Ahh!" Kowalski exclaimed when Rico was done. "Without that plus sign, it makes no sense as a schematic. Though, I question the Lunacorn."

Private clapped his fins together. "I like it!" he said.

It was done. The plan—and the world—had been saved. It was time for the Penguins to get back to the zoo before anyone noticed they were gone.

CHAPTER 6

The next day, the Penguins were safely back in their lair watching television. Today Kowalski's creation was going to be shown at the museum for the first time, and the local news was covering the event. As always, Chuck Charles was at the scene.

"We're here for the unveiling of the museum's latest acquisition," the reporter began. "The first ever created by a nonhuman."

The camera panned over to reveal Bella Bon Bueno standing next to the covered work of art.

"And now," Chuck went on, "world-famous art critic Bella Bon Bueno will do the honors."

The art critic nodded. Turning, she grasped the corner of the cover and quickly pulled. As it fell away, the "painting" was revealed. The crowd that had come for the unveiling let out *oohs* and *aahs*. But as soon as she saw the piece, Bella's nose wrinkled in disgust.

"No, no, no!" she cried. "This is not right. Something is . . . different." As she leaned in closer, the camera zoomed in as well. Suddenly, she jabbed a finger right at the Lunacorn that Rico had drawn the night before. Then as the Penguins watched in horror, she ripped a piece of the drawing off. "Amateurish forgery!" she shouted as she held the ripped paper up in front of the camera.

In the lair, Kowalski watched the events unfold on the TV screen. Then he shook his head and wiped a tear from his eye. "Critics can be so cruel," he sad sadly.

"Buck up, soldier," Skipper said, putting a flipper on Kowalski's shoulder. "You may not be recognized as a great artist, but you're a darn good inventor of devices that could save the world . . ."

"With only a fifty percent chance of destroying it," Private finished.

Kowalski straightened up. His friends were right. He did know how to make amazing inventions. This was just a small setback. There would be plenty more devices and diagrams.

He would just make sure that next time, they stayed out of the hands of pesky art critics.

///   ///   ///

Kowalski wasn't the only one getting back to work. Burt hadn't given up on his painting. Elephants have long memories. And Burt hadn't forgotten how mean Bella had been to him. He wanted to prove her wrong. So he had managed to sneak out of the zoo and make his way to the museum. Then he placed his painting on the wall. Stepping back, he admired his work.

"And they said my work would never hang in the museum," he said triumphantly.

Satisfied, Burt turned and started to leave—through a giant, elephant-sized hole in the museum wall. Unfortunately, at that very moment, the night guard was making his rounds. Passing by the hole, he did a double take. Stopping, he stared at the hole. Then at Burt. Finally, he shrugged. "Modern art," he said. "I still don't get it."

Turning, the guard left, and Burt let out a sigh of relief. That had been too close. It was time to get back to the zoo. From now on, he would leave the adventures to the Penguins.